W9-BOM-536

Snail and Buffalo

A Melanie Kroupa Book

For June and Peter—J.L.

For Emily—T.C.

Text copyright © 1995 by Jim Latimer

Illustrations copyright © 1995 by Tom Curry

All rights reserved. No part of this book may be reproduced or transmitted in any form or by any means, electronic or mechanical, including photocopying, recording, or by any information storage or retrieval system, without permission in writing from the Publisher.

Orchard Books
95 Madison Avenue
New York, NY 10016

Manufactured in the United States of America
Printed by Barton Press, Inc.   Bound by Horowitz/Rae.   Book design by Chris Hammill Paul.

10   9   8   7   6   5   4   3   2   1

The text of this book is set in 13 point Stempel Schneidler.
The illustrations are painted with an acrylic drybrush technique on hardboard.

Library of Congress Cataloging-in-Publication Data
Latimer, Jim, date.
    Snail and Buffalo / by Jim Latimer ; illustrated by Tom Curry.
        p.   cm.
    "A Melanie Kroupa book."
    Summary: Buffalo is huge, brave, and fast whereas Snail is tiny, fearful, and slow, and because of their individual differences each can do things that the other cannot.
    ISBN 0-531-09490-1. —ISBN 0-531-08790-5 (lib. bdg.)
    [1. Individuality—Fiction. 2. Snails—Fiction. 3. Bison—Fiction.] I. Curry, Tom, ill. II. title.
PZ7.L369617Sn   1995
[E]—dc20   95-4276

Snail and Buffalo

by Jim Latimer
Illustrated by Tom Curry

Orchard Books

New York

Buffalo stood under a watery sky, near a gathering of rushes and marsh grass. Buffalo was alone in the sprawling prairie wetlands, and yet he was not quite alone.

There, on a stem beside him, was a small animal—a snail.

Buffalo loomed above Snail. He was a tower, a church and a steeple in horns and brown wool. Snail stared up at him. Buffalo peered down at her. He gave his head a shake, lifted an enormous hoof, and let it fall.

"What?" he asked. "What are you?"

"Snail," said Snail.

Buffalo told Snail he was a buffalo, which she could see. He swept his tail from side to side. In the sky behind him was a promise of lightning, a feel of thunder.

"Buffalos," Buffalo informed Snail, "are big."

Buffalos were. Big enough to step on a snail. Big enough to inhale a snail. Slowly, very slowly, one quarter of an inch after one quarter of an inch, Snail began to move away.

"What?" Buffalo asked her, taking a small step to catch up. "What are you doing?"

Snail blushed. She was hurrying, moving very fast for a snail. She did not want to tell him what she was doing.

"Well," said Buffalo carelessly, taking another step, staying close, "buffalos *do* a lot of things."

Snail, still hurrying, imagined buffalos doing things, all of them dangerous to snails.

"We lick salt," Buffalo told her, "and we rub our foreheads against trees. Buffalos thrash and charge and cake their coats with mud. Buffalos eat tall grass."

There was a stand of cottonwoods and willow trees nearby.
Buffalo rubbed his forehead against a cottonwood, then rolled
and thrashed, caking his coat. And then he charged.

"We run thirty-two miles an hour," Buffalo told Snail.
"We have thirty-two teeth and we wave with our hooves."
Buffalo gave Snail a wave.

"We wave our *tails,*" he said. "Actually, it's more of a swish, what we do."

Snail turned to look. Buffalo brought his tail around. He gave it a pump—a swish. Then he planted his hooves, bent his knees, and JUMPED suddenly.

"We jump," he said. "And buffalos are *brave.*"

Buffalo told Snail that buffalos were not afraid of ghosts or witches. Snail was afraid of ghosts. She was also afraid of witches—and buffalos.

"Do snails lick salt?" Buffalo asked her.

"Snails don't," she told him.

"Do snails thrash?"

Snail dropped her head. Snails did not thrash or cake their coats. Snails did not *have* coats. They did not have thirty-two teeth, or even twenty-two, and they didn't charge. Snail could not go thirty-two miles, not in an hour or a day. Not in her whole life.

Snail's shell seemed to wilt. What did snails do? she wondered.

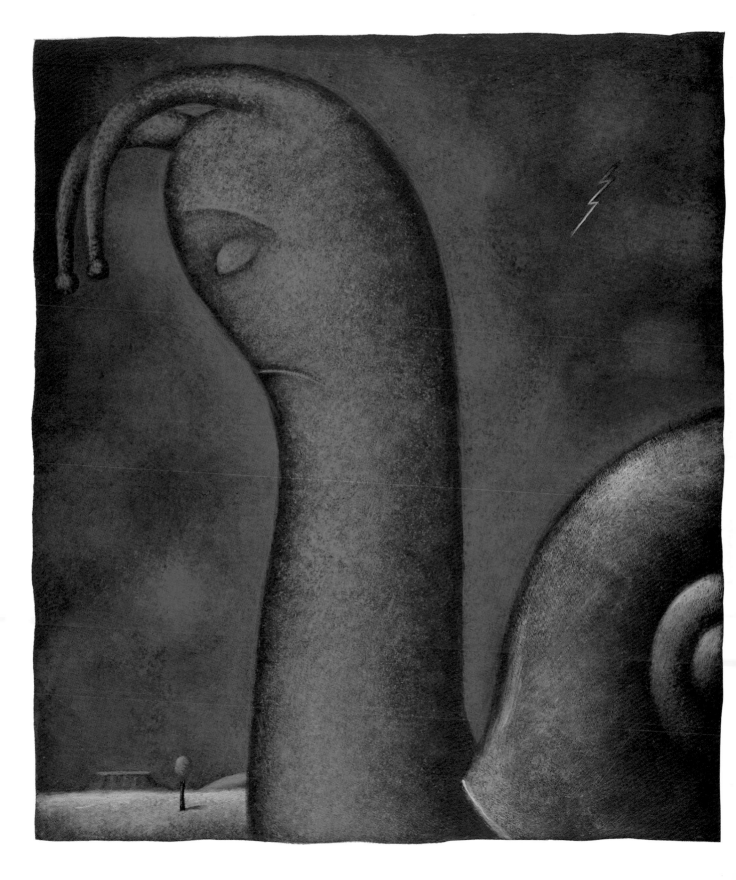

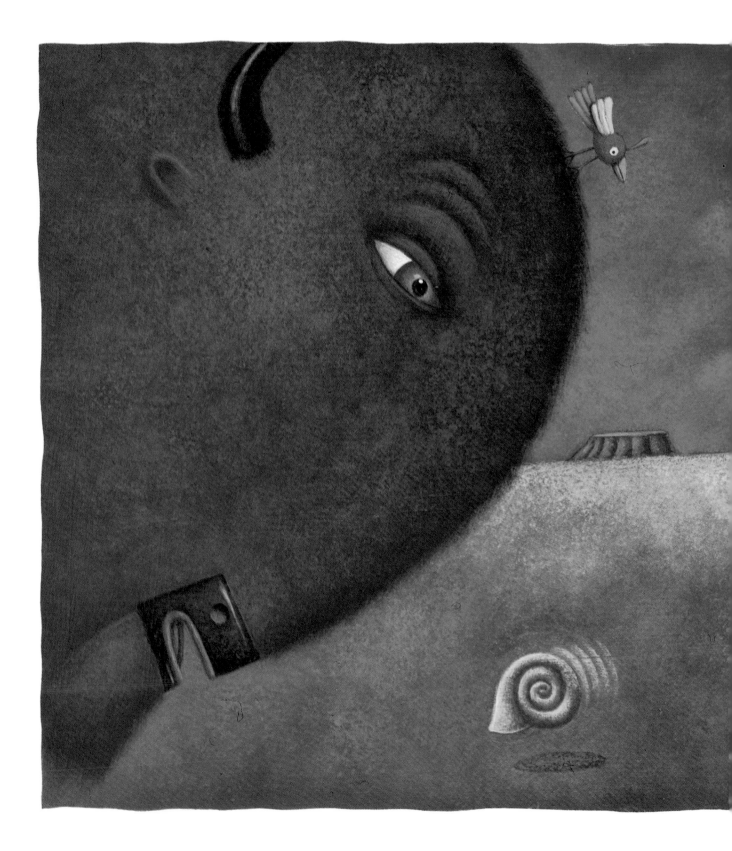

"We *whorl*," she told Buffalo finally. "That's all."

Buffalo did not know what "whorl" meant. "How do you mean?" he asked her.

Snail showed him.

Buffalo lowered his head. He knit his brow and watched as Snail's shell circled around itself, making a slow spiral.

Snail was a pinwheel, a windmill, and a barber pole. She was a slow propeller, Buffalo decided.

In his mind, Buffalo became a propeller. He planted his back hooves in the marsh grass and slowly tried to walk his front hooves around them in a circle. He planted his forehooves and slowly tried to walk his back hooves around. Buffalo tried it fast, but it was no use. He was not a propeller, slow or fast. He tripped and sat down heavily on his pump-handle tail.

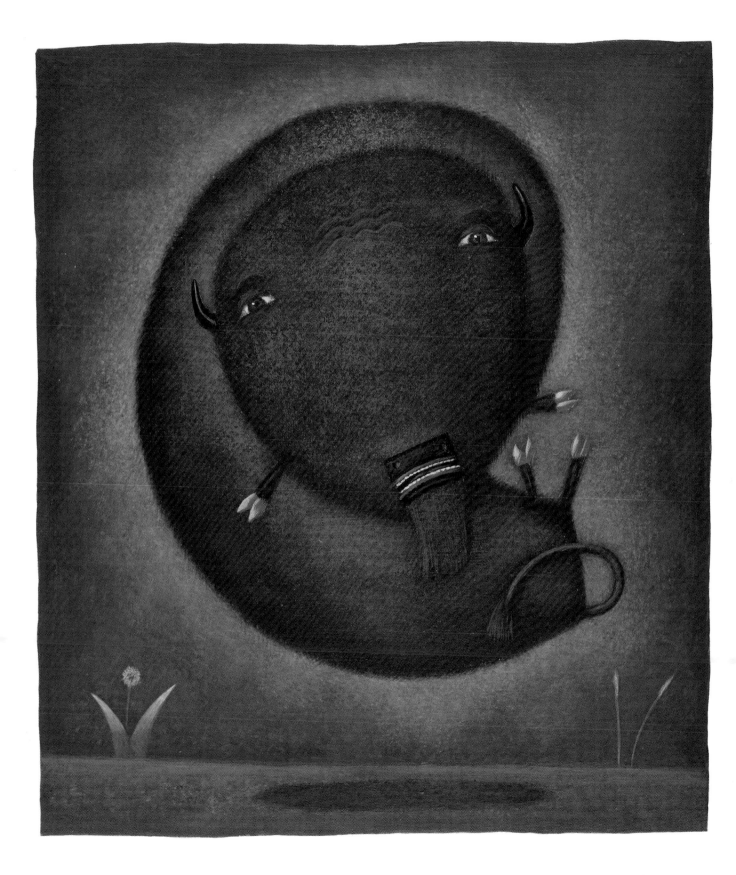

Buffalo gave Snail a sheepish look. "It looks like rain," he said.

"Snails siphon," Snail told him. She had a siphon, a kind of straw, built in. "We siphon when we drink," she said, showing Buffalo how.

Buffalo stared at his tail awhile, but, no, he doubted it could ever be a siphon.

"Snails talk to clams," Snail said. Snail could speak in Clam, in Mussel, and in Limpet—also Periwinkle. Then Snail told Buffalo she could *retract.*

As he watched, Snail seemed to disappear. Her shell toppled and rolled toward him. It struck Buffalo's hoof with a click and came to rest. Buffalo was alone. Snail had vanished.

In the distance, lightning flickered, and there was a murmur of thunder. Buffalo jumped.

Thunder startled him, he admitted. Snail reappeared suddenly. Did snails cause thunder and lightning? Buffalo wondered.

Snail told Buffalo she could walk on one foot. She asked him if he had an aquarium. "I could walk on one foot up the inside of your aquarium," she said.

Buffalo watched Snail walk on one foot up the side of a stem. He asked her to retract again. Snail disappeared into her shell and reappeared under a flickering sky—one hundred times.

Then she climbed her stem again. Compared to a buffalo on one foot, Snail was *fast.* Compared to a buffalo listening to thunder, Snail was *brave.*

Buffalo would have told her so if a reindeer had not just then stepped out of the marsh.

Reindeer, looking rough, his fur unkempt and ragged, gave Buffalo a surly greeting and glared at Snail. He reached down with his muzzle and gave her a sour sniff. "What?" he asked. "A slug? A slug wearing a seashell?"

Buffalo told Reindeer that Snail was a snail.

"Whatever," said Reindeer. "A slug's close relative." Reindeer made a sour face. "You," he informed Buffalo, "a reindeer's relative, are talking to more or less a slug."

Snail jumped from her stem into Buffalo's woolly coat.

"And—" continued Reindeer. "Where did she go?" Snail was hurrying up the side of Buffalo. Reindeer, squinting, saw her now. He gave Buffalo a mean look. "Snails are small," he said. "Snails are slow. Snails do not have hooves, for heaven's sake. Snails don't *do* anything."

During Reindeer's speech, Snail hurried on one foot across Buffalo's back.

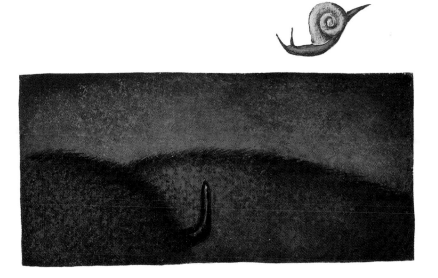

She peered out at Reindeer from between Buffalo's ears, from
between his horns. Lightning flared above her in the watery sky.
Thunder seemed to rumple the clouds. Buffalo and Reindeer
stood face to face, their noses almost touching. With Snail on
his forehead, Buffalo was not afraid. He pumped his tail and
stepped closer.

"Snails," said Buffalo, "are small. Snails do not have hooves.
They do not rub their foreheads against trees or lick salt or cake

their coats. But," Buffalo told Reindeer, "snails are *fast*. Compared to a buffalo walking on one foot, a snail is *lightning*."

The lightning crackled overhead.

"And," Buffalo concluded, "snails whorl and siphon, they talk in Clam—and they *retract*."

Snail whorled. She said "reindeer" in Clam, and then, as the thunder roared and lightning seemed to split apart the sky, she disappeared.

Reindeer blinked. He reared backward, and turned and ran. He ran away and did not come back.

Snail reappeared on Buffalo's head. Buffalo looked up, trying to see her. *Did* snails make lightning? he wondered. Buffalo gave his tail a swish, one for himself and one for Snail.

And then a small animal
in a "seashell" and a tower
and steeple in brown wool
disappeared together in
the pouring rain.